weather
everywhere

by Denise Casey

photographs by Jackie Gilmore

Macmillan Books for Young Readers ▪ *New York*

MACMILLAN BOOKS FOR YOUNG READERS
An imprint of Simon & Schuster Children's Publishing Division
Simon & Schuster Macmillan
1230 Avenue of the Americas
New York, NY 10020

The text of this book is set in 14.5 Aster
Printed and bound in Hong Kong on recycled paper
First edition

10 9 8 7 6 5 4 3 2 1

LIBRARY OF CONGRESS CATALOGING-IN-PUBLICATION DATA
Casey, Denise.
Weather everywhere / by Denise Casey;
photographs by Jackie Gilmore. — 1st ed
p. cm.
SUMMARY: An introduction to temperature,
wind, and moisture, the three primary elements
that interact to create various weather conditions.
ISBN 0-02-717777-7
1. Weather—Juvenile literature. 2. Meteorology—Juvenile literature.
[1. Weather.] I. Gilmore, Jackie, ill. II. Title.
QC981.3.C373 1995   551.5—dc20   92-23239

Many thanks to Tom Dunham, radio and TV forecaster
for Jackson Hole, Wyoming, and Fred Ostby, director of the
National Severe Storm Forecast Center, for their gracious
help in checking the accuracy of the book, and Cathy Bobak for
her watercolor illustrations.

—D. C.

Thanks to teacher Laurie Dean and the students of Garfield Elementary School
for their extensive assistance with photographing children studying weather; to
photographers Melanie Basner and Jacqui Meghani for the photographs on page 9
and pages 29 and 33, respectively; and to my numerous and cooperative family
members for their participation.

—J. G.

For my parents
—D.C.

For Christian, Kelsey, Amy, Melissa, Clinton, and Michael,
who are bright as the sun and beautiful as a rainbow
—J.G.

Weather is everywhere and it is always changing. The weather can change from hour to hour, from day to day, and from season to season. Weather is all the changing combinations of temperature, wind, and moisture in the air.

Air surrounds the earth. It is part of a thick layer of gases called the atmosphere. We cannot see the air, but we breathe it, we feel it blow against our faces, and we see it move leaves and branches on trees. When people talk about the weather, they are really talking about what is happening to this layer of air. How hot or cold is it? How windy is it? How wet is it?

Let's take a closer look.

HOW HOT OR COLD IS IT?

Our weather on earth begins far away, at the sun. The sun is a star that shines on the earth. It warms the air and everything on the earth, including the land and water.

The longer the sun shines on a place, the warmer the temperature becomes. In summer, the sun shines for many hours every day and the heat builds up. In winter, the sun only shines for a short time every day, so less heat builds up.

Even though it is evening, the air stays warm enough in summer for outdoor activities such as picnics and ball games.

The equator is an imaginary line around the middle of the earth. It is hot at the equator because the sun shines for many hours every day and is directly overhead nearly all year long. The sun's rays feel hottest when the sun is directly overhead.

If you traveled north from the equator, every day you would get less direct sunlight. So, overall, each new day would be a little cooler than the last. Finally, you would arrive at the North Pole, where it's always cold because very little direct sunlight hits the top of the earth. If you traveled south from the equator, you would arrive at the South Pole, where it's also very cold. So, in a general way, you can tell what kind of temperature you'll have by where you live in relation to the equator.

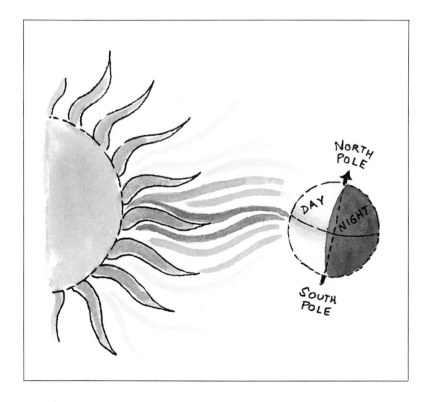

This is not a picture of a sunrise or a sunset. It is the sun shining in the middle of the night. At the North Pole, the sun does not set from March to September. This area is always cold, even with the "midnight sun," because the sunlight is indirect.

The temperature often follows a pattern throughout the year, as it changes with the seasons. The seasons change because the earth is tilted slightly as it orbits the sun. We say that it tilts on an axis, an imaginary line from the North Pole to the South Pole.

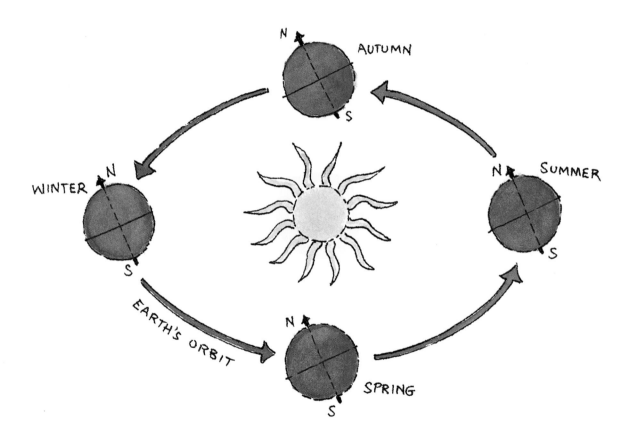

During part of the earth's orbit, the North Pole tilts toward the sun. During the opposite part of the orbit, it tilts away.

When the North Pole is tilted toward the sun, the northern half of the earth gets the most direct rays of sunlight. This direct sunlight feels hot. Now it is summer in the northern half of the world.

When the North Pole is tilted away from the sun, it is winter in the northern half of the world. The sun's rays hit at an extreme angle, spreading out over a large area. Winter sunlight may be very bright, but it does not feel as warm as summer sunlight.

There are other reasons why some parts of the earth are warmer than others. For one thing, dark-colored places heat up more quickly than light-colored ones. The earth has many different colors of soil, rock, plants, and water. They all heat up at different rates and hold the heat for different lengths of time.

Another reason why temperatures vary is that land heats up and cools down more quickly than water does. You can see this for yourself. Fill one dish with water and another with dry soil, both about the same temperature. Place them in the sun together. After fifteen minutes, which one feels warmer? Try putting them in a refrigerator for fifteen minutes. Which one is cooler?

The closer air is to the surface of the earth, the warmer it is. It is cooler on top of a building than it is at ground level, and it is even cooler on top of a mountain. That is why there is snow on top of mountains, even when the air at ground level is warm.

HOW WINDY IS IT?

Differences in temperature cause the earth's air to move, but air doesn't move in random directions. Hot air rises and cold air falls. When warm air rises, cooler air moves in to replace the rising hot air. This is one reason why enormous currents of air flow around the earth in the same general patterns all the time. Moving air is wind.

The wind that frequently blows across the water makes sailboating a popular hobby.

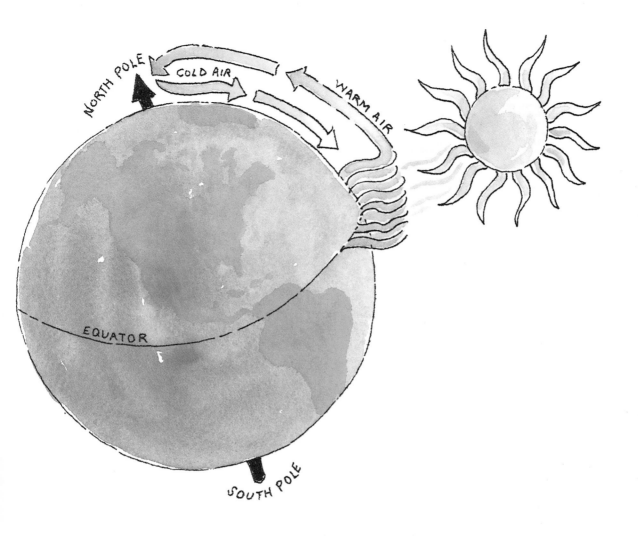

Because hot air rises and cold air falls and warm air is lighter than cold air, the weight of the air pressing down on the equator is less than the weight of the cold, heavier air pressing down at the poles. This is why we say there is low pressure at the equator and high pressure at the poles. Air moves from cold high-pressure areas to warm low-pressure areas.

The wind's speed and direction are affected by its having to go up over mountains, down into valleys, through forests, between buildings, or across vast plains.

The rock formations in this canyon can make the wind shift many times as it blows through. But where the land is flat and clear, the wind can blow steadily.

Wind is an important part of the weather system. As it circles the earth, it carries heat from hot places to cold ones. It also carries moisture from wet areas to dry ones.

The little bit of rain that falls in a desert may have been carried from an ocean or lake miles away.

HOW WET IS IT?

As wind blows around the world, it passes over water in oceans, lakes, and rivers. Heat from the sun causes the liquid water to change to a gas, called water vapor. We say the water evaporates into the air. Air that has water vapor in it is moist, or humid. Warm air can hold more water vapor than cool air can.

Nearly three-fourths of the earth's surface is covered with water. Water is found in oceans, lakes, rivers, and smaller bodies of water.

Even if you can't see humidity, you can feel it. Some days feel dry and comfortable. Other days feel muggy and sticky—it depends on how much water vapor is in the air.

If you want to feel the difference between dry air and humid air, fill a sink with hot water. Hold your face over the water but don't touch the water. Notice how the air feels. Soon your face feels wet. It's because water vapor has risen into the air.

Wind carries water vapor high above the earth. As the moist air rises and cools, the water vapor condenses, changing back to water droplets. When the air is very cold, the water vapor turns into tiny ice crystals. Billions of water droplets or ice crystals hanging together in the air are clouds.

Watching clouds can help you predict what kind of weather is coming. For instance, when you first see thin, cirrus clouds high in the sky, and then over the next day or two, stratus clouds that grow thicker and lower, you can be pretty sure that rain will fall soon.

There are three main types of clouds. Puffy clouds are called cumulus.

Wispy clouds are cirrus.

Flat clouds are stratus.

Water is constantly changing from water drops to water vapor and back again. The same water that falls as rain one day may trickle into a river the next day and eventually flow into an ocean. It may move thousands of miles in the ocean's currents for months or even years. That same water then may evaporate and continue moving around the earth with the wind. Finally, it may condense in a cloud and fall to earth again as rain or snow. This is the earth's water cycle.

As air around clouds cools, more and more water vapor condenses into water droplets. The tiny droplets bump against one another, join together into bigger water drops, and eventually fall to earth as rain. If the raindrops fall through a layer of cold air near the ground, they freeze into little pellets of ice called sleet.

When the air temperature is below freezing, the moisture in clouds turns to ice crystals. As they fall, they stick to one another and become larger and heavier. By the time they reach the ground, they have grown into lacy, six-sided snowflakes.

There is still a lot of moisture in the air after a rainstorm. When the sun shines through the water droplets hanging in the air, it makes a rainbow. Rainbows appear in the mist of a waterfall, too. You may even be able to see one in the spray of a garden hose.

Would you like to be inside a cloud? You are, when it's foggy. Fog is what we call a cloud that touches the ground. Fog happens when warm, moist air flows over cool ground. A layer of air just above the ground is also cooled, and its water vapor condenses into droplets so small that they float in the air.

Little balls of ice, called hailstones, sometimes fall during thunderstorms. Hailstones form when frozen raindrops fall through cold air. Water droplets freeze onto their surfaces, coating them with many layers of ice. Sometimes hailstones are swept up by strong winds into cold air currents again and again. Each time, another layer of ice builds up.

When sunlight shines through ice crystals hanging in the air, it makes a bright spot appear in the sky next to the sun. This is called a sun dog.

Weather is a powerful force. Constant exposure to wind and rain can wear mountains down over time. Weather determines what kinds of plants and animals can live in different places on earth. It provides energy for people through windmills and solar collectors. As the weather changes, the world we live in also changes.

Directly or indirectly, all living things need air, water, and sunlight to live. Weather is everywhere you go!

GLOSSARY

air	a colorless, odorless gas that is a part of the earth's atmosphere
air currents	large "rivers" of air that flow around the earth in the same general patterns
air pressure	the weight of the air pressing down on the earth
atmosphere	the thick layer of gases surrounding the earth
axis	an imaginary line connecting the North and South Poles
cloud	a mass of water droplets or ice crystals clinging together; *cirrus* clouds are wispy, *cumulus* clouds are puffy, *stratus* clouds are flat
condense	to change from a gas to liquid
direct sunlight	light that hits the earth from high overhead; direct sunlight is stronger than **indirect sunlight**
equator	an imaginary line around the middle of the earth, halfway between the North and South Poles
evaporate	to change from a liquid to gas
fog	a cloud that touches the ground
hailstones	little balls of ice that fall from clouds like rain

humid	damp or moist
humidity	the wetness or dampness of air
ice	the frozen, solid form of water
indirect sunlight	sunlight that shines on the earth at a very low angle; indirect sunlight is weaker than **direct sunlight**
midnight sun	the sun when it appears above the horizon at midnight; this happens only near the poles
moisture	wetness
North Pole	the most northern point on earth
orbit	to move in a circular path around a central object; the earth orbits the sun
rain	water droplets that form in clouds and fall to earth
rainbow	a colorful arc that appears when sunlight shines through water droplets
season	one of four parts of the year; the four seasons are spring, summer, autumn (or fall), and winter
sleet	frozen rain
snow	six-sided crystals of ice that fall from clouds like rain
solar collector	a device that absorbs the sun's heat energy
South Pole	the most southern point on earth
summer	the season when days are longest and temperatures are generally warmest

sun	the star around which the earth and other planets orbit; the sun gives heat and light energy to the planets
sun dog	a bright spot in the sky caused by sunlight shining through ice crystals
temperature	a measure of hotness or coldness
thunderstorm	a storm with thunder and lightning
vapor	liquid in a gas form, usually mist or steam
weather	all the changing combinations of temperature, wind, and moisture
wind	air moving over the ground
winter	the season when days are shortest and temperatures are generally coolest